For

Lulu

C. Spliedt

10 9 8 7 6 5 4 3 2 1
ISBN-13: 978-1490324579
ISBN-10: 1490324577

Edited by Elizabeth Mazza
Edited again by G.W. Mercure
Designed by C. Spliedt

Thank you to everyone who has helped make this book possible.

www.runrabbitproductions.com

How Do The Animals Live?

Written & Illustrated by

C. Spliedt

Hi, my name is Lulu, and I love to explore.
I've explored my whole house, from ceiling to floor.
Mom doesn't mind, she thinks that I should:
curiosity's a gift, she says, so long as I'm good.

Outside in my yard I see the plants and the trees,
I smell all the flowers, I follow the bees.
The squirrels and bunnies: how they hop and they crawl!
It's the animals' homes I like to explore most of all.

The bluebird I see flying up through the air:
Oh how would it be to live way up there?
Living up in a tree, I wonder, would that be strange?
I could try it, perhaps: it would be a nice change
to see how she lives, I could go where she stays
and to live like a bird for part of the day.

Yes, I could visit the birds, in their birdnest.
Way up in a tree, I would be their guest.
They sing and they chirp and they fly all around.
It would be so much fun, so far from the ground.
A girl in a nest, that might sound absurd,
But I'll do it, you'll see, I'll live like a bird.
But what's that for lunch? I see something that squirms!
You're really quite nice, but I don't eat worms!

I could travel around and see other lands:
I would go to a place where the ground is all sand.
I'd visit a lizard who soaks in the sun.
In the desert we'd play and we'd have lots of fun.
With his thick scaly skin as tough as a bone,
if the sun gets too hot, he hides under a stone.
But it's hard to find water, or a nice shady spot.
You're really quite nice, but it's just way too hot!

This porcupine here I would follow around.
We'd stroll and we'd wander, the forest abounds.
She has hundreds of quills all over her back
each one of them long, and as sharp as a tack.
I think that she's charming, not bossy or smug,
although I do hope she won't ask for a hug.
But I can't get too close, I don't want to sound whiny,
you're really quite nice, but those spines are too spiny!

Then I'd visit some bats, yes I'd go to a cave.
It's cold and it's dark, so I'd have to be brave.
I'm not too scared to climb, so up I would go
They fly up to perch, but I have to go slow.
They use sonar to guide them, it's too dark to see,
as they fly through the night on their bug-eating spree.
But from here my smile looks like a frown.
You're really quite nice, but it's just too upside down!

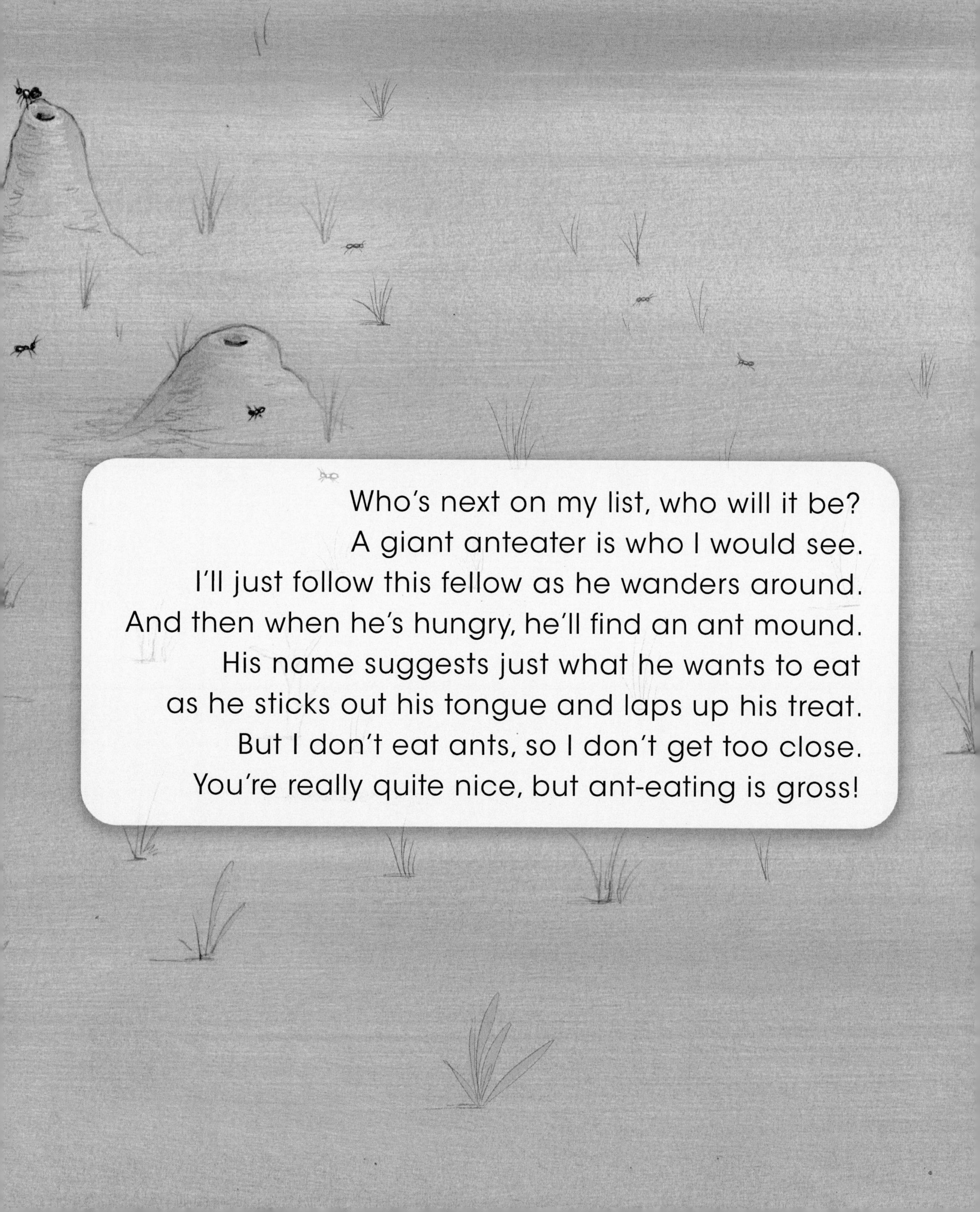

Who's next on my list, who will it be?
A giant anteater is who I would see.
I'll just follow this fellow as he wanders around.
And then when he's hungry, he'll find an ant mound.
His name suggests just what he wants to eat
as he sticks out his tongue and laps up his treat.
But I don't eat ants, so I don't get too close.
You're really quite nice, but ant-eating is gross!

Oh the places I'll travel and what fun it will be!
Now what's next on my journey, just who will I see?
I'll go visit some goats that live way, way up high
on the tops of the mountains that reach into the sky.
They balance on rocks and they don't ever fall.
They jump and they play on those mountains so tall.
But for me to get up there takes so much time.
You're really quite nice, but there's too much to climb!

For my next destination I am bringing a light,
as I must venture down where it's darker than night.
I'll go under the ground, deep down in a hole
where I'll visit my friend the little brown mole.
He's got big claws for digging, but his eyes are so small.
Yet he gets where he's going with no trouble at all.
But for me it's too dark, and I can't hear a sound.
You're really quite nice, but it's too underground!

I know what I'll do! I will visit a beaver
as she's chopping down trees with her teeth like a cleaver.
She's making a dam with all of those sticks,
and it stops up the water, it's stronger than bricks.
I can help with her work, but I just have to say
that my teeth are not sharp, so it might take all day.
My mouth hurts when I chomp, but she does it with ease.
You're really quite nice, but I can't bite down trees!

Well...I guess that I could visit a skunk.
Though I've heard they give off a terrible funk.
Unlike me, they come out mostly at night,
so I'll stay up really late—I hope that's all right.
They're really quite cute, despite their strong stench.
If the smell gets too bad, my nose I will clench.
But it goes through my nose right down to my belly.
You're really quite nice, but you're just way too smelly!

I'll visit the north, with my friend polar bear.
I'll dress nice and warm, as there's snow everywhere.
He's so powdery white, and so big and so furry,
he blends in with the ice, when the snow starts to flurry.
My house is so warm, while he sleeps in the snow.
He must wear his fur coat wherever he goes.
But my teeth start to chatter, my nose runs, I'm sneezing.
You're really quite nice, but I must go, I'm freezing!

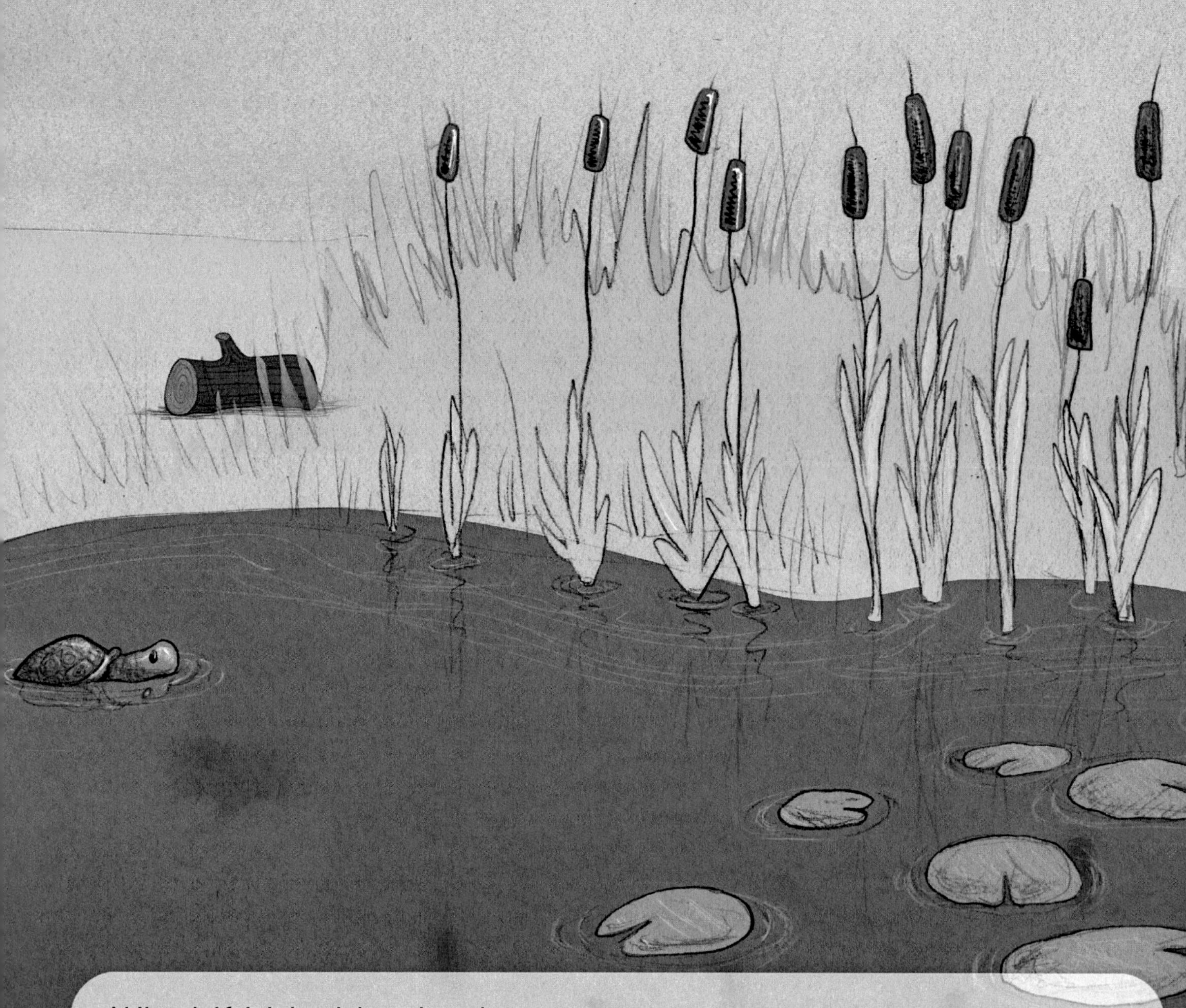

What if I tried to stay in a swamp
where the crocodiles swim and they wait and they chomp!
Those big scaly beasts, they have nothing to do
so I'll jump in the water and I'll sit with them, too.
I hope they don't mind as I settle right in.
Oh what a fun time this journey has been,
as I'm soaking in here with these crocs that I've met:
You're really quite nice, but I'm getting too wet!

I've learned so much about my animal friends
but now it seems that my journey must end.
Of all of the places I've been on my quest,
I have decided that I like my home the best.
So I've come up with a plan, I'll have to say please,
but it's a really good plan, I hope mom agrees:
Since I think that my home's such a nice place to be
I'll invite all the animals to come live with me!

Made in the USA
Middletown, DE
15 January 2015